To Albert,
With all my love,
—Laurie

For little Juliette, my fashion princess
and best shopping buddy
—J.K.

Mallory and Mary Ann Take New York

by Laurie Friedman

illustrations by Jennifer Kalis

darbycreek

MINNEAPOLIS

CONTENTS

A WORD FROM MALLORY

My name is Mallory McDonald, like the restaurant but no relation. Age ten and a half.

Even though I'm only ten and a half, I've spent a lot of time, especially lately, thinking about what I want to be when I grow up.

I'll get to the "especially lately" part in a minute, but first, I want to talk about what I want to be when I grow up.

I'll start by telling you what I don't want to be.

I don't want to be a truck driver or a dermatologist (that's a doctor in charge of getting rid of pimples—ew). I also don't want to be a professional ice-skater (I'm terrible at ice-skating), a math teacher (I'm also terrible at math), or a zookeeper. The only animal I want to take care of is my cat, Cheeseburger.

I DO want to be an ice-cream scooper, a hairdresser, an astronaut, or a movie star. But there's something I want to be even more than all those things. I would LOVE to be a fashion designer.

I've been thinking a lot lately about being a fashion designer. (Remember how I said I would talk about the "especially lately" part later?)

The reason is that my favorite TV show, hosted by my favorite TV hostess, Fashion Fran, is about to have a fashion design contest for kids. I don't know a lot about the contest yet. But after today, I'll know a whole lot more.

Fashion Fran is going to announce the details of her contest on this afternoon's episode. My best friend, Mary Ann, and I have been waiting forever to find out what this contest is all about. The good news is we don't have to wait much longer.

Fashion Fran starts soon!

And we can hardly wait!

A CONTEST

"Hurry up! Fran is on in five!" I say into the phone.

"Get the popcorn and lemonade ready," Mary Ann says back. "I'll be right over with pens and paper."

One of the best parts about living next door to my best friend is that it doesn't take long to get to each other's houses. Mary Ann is on my couch before I even get there with the snacks.

Fashion Fran is about to announce the details of her fashion design contest that she has been talking about for weeks.

I turn on the TV and settle in next to Mary Ann.

She takes a sip of her lemonade. "I don't think I can wait another second," she says.

I shake my head. I agree completely. Fran announced the contest a few weeks ago, but it feels like it has taken months for it to officially begin. And today's the day. I can't wait to find out what it's all about.

As the music we've been listening to every afternoon for as long as I can remember starts to play, Mary Ann and I squeal.

Like always, we count down with the announcer as we wait for Fran to appear on the screen. "The moment we've been waiting for is finally here!" I say.

But before we get to enjoy it, my brother, Max, walks into the room. He grabs the remote and changes the channel.

"I want to see the sports scores," he says.

Mary Ann and I both fly off the couch at the same time. So does the bowl of popcorn. My brother is usually faster than I am, but today I grab the remote out of his hand before he can stop me.

"Are you crazy?!?" I shout at Max. "Mary Ann and I have a V.I.S. to watch."

Max looks at me like he has no idea what I'm talking about, so I explain. "V.I.S. is short for *Very Important Show*." I tell him that Fashion Fran is having a design contest. "We're going to find out all of the details today!"

Now Max looks at me like I'm the one

who is crazy. "And you and Birdbrain actually think you can win?"

I wave my hand at Max to make him stop talking.

A. I don't like when he calls my best friend Birdbrain.

B. His question is ridiculous. We have as good a chance as anybody.

C. I don't have time to answer anyway. Fran is starting to talk.

Mary Ann and I both put our fingers to our lips and make a *shhh!* sound. But Max is already leaving. Mary Ann and I turn our attention to the TV.

"Fashionable viewers, welcome to a very special episode of the show." Fran smiles at the camera. She pats down her already smooth hair. Then she twirls so viewers can see what she's wearing.

"I love her sparkly sweater," I say.

"And her lace skirt," says Mary Ann.

We both shake our heads. One thing Mary Ann and I have always agreed on is that Fran is very fashionable.

The camera pans over the audience. It is filled with happy faces. "Can you even imagine what it would be like to be there?" I ask Mary Ann.

Mary Ann squeezes my arm.

It has always been our dream to be on her show together. But it is hard to imagine that ever happening. We watch as Fran keeps talking. "I'm sure you are all

anxious to hear about the design contest," says Fran. "But first, I want to tell you a little bit about how I started as a fashion designer."

I turn up the volume. I know Mary Ann wants to hear this as much as I do.

Fran tells viewers how she loved playing with fabrics and designing outfits when she was a little girl. The camera cuts to pictures of ten-year-old Fran using a miniature sewing machine she says her grandmother gave her.

"I have been sewing and designing ever since." Fran smiles into the camera. "Now, it is your turn."

"The contest is simple," says Fran. "Design your dream outfit, your most perfect, fashionable ensemble, on one sheet of 8½ by 11 paper. Please use pencils and colored pencils only. Send your design to my studio in New York, addressed to Design Your Dream Outfit Contest."

A New York City address flashes on the front of the screen.

"Write that down," I say to Mary Ann.

Mary Ann starts writing.

Fran keeps talking. "You have three weeks to submit your design. I will personally look at each and every one that comes in." Lights twinkle on the screen behind Fran. She smiles into the camera. "And when we come back, I'll announce the prize for winning the Design Your Dream Outfit contest."

The TV cuts to a commercial.

"I can't wait to start designing," says Mary Ann. "Me too," I say to my best friend. My head starts filling up with ideas. I can already picture the dream outfits Mary Ann and I are going to design.

I'm really excited to design my dream outfit. But I'm even more excited to find out what you get if you win the contest.

When Fran returns, the lights twinkle
again. "Now, the moment you have all
been waiting for." A drum rolls in the
background.

I squeeze Mary Ann's hand as Fran starts
talking.

Fran raises an eyebrow and grins.
"Viewers, I will choose the winning design.
Then our seamstresses will sew it, creating
a real dream outfit from the design." Fran
pauses like what she's about to say next is
the most exciting thing she has said so far.
Mary Ann and I lean in toward the TV.

"The winner will receive an all-expenses-
paid trip for four to New York City . . . AND
a chance to appear on my show and model
the winning design!"

When Fran says that, Mary Ann starts
bouncing up and down on the couch. I'm
starting to feel couch-sick. It's the same

thing as seasick, except it happens when you're on a couch that is moving instead of a boat.

"Wow! Wow! Wow!" screams Mary Ann. "All we have to do is win the contest, and we get to go to New York City and model our outfits on the *Fashion Fran* show. We're going on *Fashion Fran!*"

I look at Mary Ann. I've never seen her so bouncy. I'm excited too, but I'm not sure why she's so bouncy. I'm also not sure why she used the word "we."

I put my hand on her arm and she stops moving. "Didn't you hear Fran?" I say. "She didn't say *"winners,"* she said *"winner."*

I wait for what I said to sink in, but it doesn't. Mary Ann waves at me like she's heard enough. She points to the screen. Fran is starting to talk again.

She holds up a sketch pad and a pencil.

"You design it. Our seamstresses sew it. One lucky winner will model her design on the show." Fran smiles. "This contest is only open for the next three weeks. So get busy drawing your dream outfit. I know there's a fashion designer in all of you."

Fran blows a kiss and waves. "That's it for today. See you tomorrow with more of the latest, greatest finds in the world of fashion."

The camera cuts to another commercial.

"*One lucky winner*" keeps spinning through my head. What was supposed to be the most exciting episode ever just turned into the worst episode ever. "What are we going to do?" I ask Mary Ann.

Mary Ann looks at me funny. "About what?"

Sometimes I wonder what goes on in Mary Ann's brain.

Is it working?

Mary Ann's brain

"Only one person gets to go on Fran's show. And there are two of us."

Mary Ann takes a deep *give-me-a-minute-to-think-about-this* breath. "It's simple," she says. "All we have to do is make a pinky swear. If one of us wins, we'll figure out a way to both go on the show."

She holds up her pinky like she's waiting for me to hook mine around hers.

I look at her. "How are we going to do that?"

Mary Ann shakes her head like now I'm the one who doesn't get it. "We need to stop talking and start promising!"

I shake my head. "I don't see how . . ."

I was going to say that I don't see how we could figure out something as big as both getting on the show, but Mary Ann stops me. She hooks my pinky in hers and shakes them up and down.

"Mallory, don't worry," she says. "Everything will work out fine. It always does when we make a pinky swear."

I nod. I try to imagine Mary Ann and me in New York. Seeing the sights. Modeling on the *Fashion Fran* show. But it's hard.

I know we made a pinky swear. But this time, I'm just not sure that's going to make everything work out.

CRUNCH TIME

I don't know why I was so worried about what happens if one of us wins the Design Your Dream Outfit contest. So far, it doesn't look like either one of us is going to win this contest.

It has been exactly two weeks and four days since Fashion Fran announced her Design Your Dream Outfit contest. For the last two weeks and four days, I have been designing outfits and Mary

Ann has been designing outfits.

We have been working on our designs every afternoon after school and on the weekends. We've hardly left my room.

The problem is . . . so far, none of our outfits look very dreamy.

Now it's crunch time. We only have three days to go before the contest is over.

I rip a sheet of paper out of the sketch pad I've been drawing in and crumple it into a ball. I toss it toward the trash can next to my desk. It misses and lands on my floor, next to the large pile of other wadded-up papers already on my floor.

Mary Ann leans back against the pillows on my bed and blows a piece of hair off her forehead. She tosses her sketch pad on the ground. "I give up."

"C'mon. We can't give up." I rub my head, which is what I do when I'm doing my most serious thinking. "We need to focus," I say.

Mary Ann snorts. "We've been focusing. I'm sick of focusing."

I pick up her sketch pad and hand it back to her. "Let's give it one more try. We just need to design the perfect outfit that we both would want to wear."

Mary Ann nods like she'll try, but she's not as into it as she was two weeks and four days ago.

I hand her a pencil, and we both flip to clean pages in our sketchbooks.

I really want to do a good job. I really want to win this contest.

I draw a model body. Then I put a pair of skinny jeans on the model.

Mary Ann looks over at my drawing. "Those look good," she says. She draws a long skirt on her model.

I don't love long skirts, but maybe Mary Ann will draw something cute on top.

"Your turn," she says.

I look at the jeans I drew. I draw a tunic top with flowing sleeves. I add little bits of lace around the neck and wrists.

"Nice!" says Mary Ann. She draws a vest with fringe to go above the skirt.

25

"Like it?" she asks.

I purse my lips and rub my head. "I'm not sure I do."

I'm trying to decide what it is that I don't like about it, but Mary Ann waves her hand at me. She doesn't seem to care if I like it or not. "Keep drawing," says Mary Ann. I can tell all she wants to do is finish the designs.

I add an armful of bracelets and a beaded necklace to my drawing.

Mary Ann adds a studded belt to hers.

I add some boots.

Mary Ann adds ballet flats.

I look at my drawing. I'm really happy with it. I hold it up so Mary Ann can get a good look. "What do you think?" I ask. I wait for Mary Ann to smile and say she loves it.

But Mary Ann frowns. "I don't know," she says. "Something is missing."

I study the model I drew. Part of me thinks Mary Ann doesn't like my drawing because I said I didn't like hers. But another part of me agrees with her. Something is definitely missing.

Suddenly I have a great idea. I add a big cowboy hat, oversized sunglasses, and long hair with bangs.

"Does hair count as part of the outfit?" Mary Ann asks.

"It's a wig!" I explain.

Mary Ann frowns again. "I don't know. I'm not sure I like the hat and the glasses. Do you really think you need all that?"

I study my design for a long time.

"I *really* think I need it," I say to Mary Ann. I'm not sure why, but I just have a feeling I do.

"OK," Mary Ann finally says like she's still not 100% sure she agrees with me, but she'll go along with it anyway.

I smile at her. "I guess I'm done!"

"Me too!" says Mary Ann.

I study her design. It's good, but it could use a little something extra. "Do you think *you* need to add something else?" I ask.

outfit by
Mallory McDonald

- cowboy hat
- Sunglasses
- wig with long straight hair
- chunky necklace
- Long flowy sleeves
- Bracelets
- Tunic top with lace edges
- Skinny jeans
- boots

Mary Ann shakes her head like her design is fine the way it is. She takes a coffee mug of colored pencils off of my desk and hands it to me. "Time to start coloring."

When we're done, we write our names and addresses on top of our designs and slip them carefully into envelopes. Then we add stamps and lick them shut.

We carefully copy Fran's address on the outside of our envelopes.

I take a deep breath. I'm tired, but I'm excited too. "I guess we're finished," I say.

Mary Ann shakes her head. "Not yet. We still have one more thing to do."

She pulls me by my arm as she walks outside. She stops in front of my mailbox.

"Put it in," says Mary Ann.

I take a deep breath. "Do you think there's any chance one of us will win?" I'm sure a lot of people are entering this contest.

Mary Ann looks at me like a teacher looking down at a student over the rim of her glasses, even though she isn't wearing any. "I think we have as good a chance as anybody."

She takes the envelope out of my hand and lays both envelopes carefully in the mailbox. "We'll never know if we don't send them in," says Mary Ann. Then she crosses her fingers for luck. "Off they go," she says with a smile.

I cross my fingers too. "Off they go," I say back.

Then I plop down on the ground. Now all we have to do is wait and see what happens.

THE ENVELOPE, PLEASE

Fact #1: For the past four weeks, Mary Ann and I have been spending a lot of time by our mailboxes.

Fact #2: My brother, Max, says all the time we've been spending by our mailboxes has been wasted time. He says there's no way either one of us is going to win any contest.

Fact #3: George, the mail carrier,

arrives in approximately ten minutes.

"Hopefully today will be our lucky day," says Mary Ann. She plops down on the ground under my mailbox.

I plop down beside her. We've been waiting so long to get a letter from Fashion Fran saying one of us won the Design Your Dream Outfit contest. At first, I was worried about what would happen if one of us won. Now, I just hope one of us does. I'm sure we could figure out a way to both go on the show. I really want today to be our lucky day, but maybe my brother is right. Maybe we aren't going to win anything.

Mary Ann grabs my arm and points down the street. "Here comes George!"

He stops his truck in front of our house. "Good afternoon, girls." George smiles at us and pulls out a stack of mail. He hands it to me. He hands the next pile to Mary Ann.

When Mary Ann and I first started waiting, we told George what we were waiting for. For the first few weeks, he stayed while we

looked through the mail to see if we got anything from Fashion Fran.

I guess George got sick of waiting, because he doesn't stay anymore.

After George drives off, Mary Ann and I start looking through our piles of envelopes.

Boring . . . lots of ads and bills. Mary Ann leans over my shoulder. "Nothing in mine. Did you get anything?" she asks.

I shake my head from side to side.

"Just plain envelopes." I keep flipping through the stack. When I flip to a shiny gold envelope, I stop. There's something different about this envelope.

Mary Ann leans in like she senses there is something different too.

I drop the rest of the mail I'm holding and turn the envelope over. Mary Ann and I both see a New York City return address.

"It's addressed to Miss Mallory McDonald." My voice is barely a whisper.

"Mallory, open it!" I can tell Mary Ann is trying to stay calm, but her voice sounds shaky.

I carefully pull back the flap on the envelope. Mary Ann and I both hold our breath as I pull out a thick sheet of gold paper. I'm almost too scared to look. Mary Ann grabs my arm. Slowly, I unfold the paper and start reading.

FROM THE DESK OF

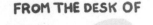

Fashion Fran

Dear Miss Mallory McDonald,

Congratulations!

You are the official winner of the Fashion Fran Design Your Dream Outfit contest. You have been selected from thousands of applicants to visit the set of my show in New York City! Our seamstresses will create your dream outfit, and you will have the opportunity to model it on a very special episode of Fashion Fran.

It is my pleasure to invite you and three others of your choosing to come to New York for three days.

You will all fly in comfort and stay at a luxury hotel in New York City as my guests. Enjoy seeing the famous sights of the city that never sleeps! My staff will ensure that your trip to New York and your time on camera is an experience you will always remember.

Enclosed is another letter for your parents with travel details and the name and number of my assistant who will help with the arrangements. Congratulations again! I love your dreamy design!

I can't wait to meet you!

Fashionably,

Fran

"You won!" Mary Ann grabs me. She starts screaming and jumping. "You won! You won! You won!"

I would scream and jump too, but I'm too shocked to scream or jump. I can't believe I won.

When Mary Ann stops screaming, I unfold the letter to my parents. I start reading it out loud. Lots of stuff about hotels, plane tickets, addresses, and dates.

"Forget that!" says Mary Ann. "You won and *we* get to be on the *Fashion Fran* show!"

Mary Ann is my lifelong best friend.

We do everything together.

We paint our toenails the same color.

We chew the same kind of gum.

We like the same TV show.

We wear matching pajamas.

We say things three times.

We've gone together on vacations and to summer camp.

And we have a pile of scrapbooks that we made together.

I have always done everything with Mary Ann. We have lived next door to each other almost all of our lives. The first pinky swear we ever made was when we swore to always be lifelong best friends. I love Mary Ann with all my heart, but sometimes she says things that scare me.

And this is one of those times.

She taps me on the shoulder like she is talking and wants my full attention.

"You won the contest, and we get to be on the *Fashion Fran* show!" This time when she says "we," she holds up her pinky like she wants to make sure I remember the pinky swear we made:

"If one of us wins, we'll figure out the rest."

"I don't see how we're going to pull this off," I say to Mary Ann. My voice is almost a whisper.

Mary Ann crosses her arms across her chest and shakes her head like she's disappointed she even has to explain this to me.

"Mallory, when we were five, we made a pinky swear that we would share all our Halloween candy.

"Even though I got two pumpkins full of candy and you only got one, I shared all my candy with you.

"I kept my pinky swear!"

Mary Ann keeps talking. "When we were seven and you were scared to go to school, we made a pinky swear that we would sit next to each other in class no matter what.

"I was the one who had to convince mean, scary Mrs. Barton to put our desks next to each other.

"I kept my pinky swear!"

Mary Ann keeps talking like she's nowhere near done. "And when we were nine, we made a pinky swear to always paint our toenails the same color.

"There have been times when I didn't like the color you picked. But I painted my toenails the same color as yours. I KEPT MY PINKY SWEAR!"

Mary Ann gives me a what-kind-of-best-friend-would-you-be-if-you-didn't-keep-your-pinky-swear look.

"A pinky swear is a pinky swear," she says.

I take a deep breath. I know a pinky swear is a pinky swear.

I just don't know how I'm going to keep this one.

OPERATION:
MOMS

Mary Ann sits on a bench while I pace
back and forth in front of the wish pond at
the end of our street. Mary Ann reads from
a clipboard.

"List?"

"Check," I say.

"Letters and pictures?"

"Check. Check."

"Folding Chairs? TV table? Back pillows?"

"Check. Check. Check."

"Cupcakes? Lemonade? Fruit Platter? Mints?"

"Check. Check. Check. And . . . check," I say.

Mary Ann takes a deep breath. "OK. We're ready to put *Operation: Moms* into action."

We both cross our fingers and our toes. Then we pick up rocks and toss them into the wish pond. Hopefully, our crossing and tossing will bring us good luck. Right now, we could really use some good luck.

Operation: Moms is going to be a tricky one. We have to convince our moms that the four people who should go to New York are Mom, me, Mary Ann, and her mom. My mom is going to say Max and Dad should go. Mary Ann's mom is going to say she's not sure it is a good idea since she is pregnant.

"I'll get the moms. You get the

blindfolds," says Mary Ann.

I nod. Then I take one last look at everything we set up. It looks good. But still, convincing our moms to take us both to New York won't be easy.

When I see Mary Ann walking down the street with our moms, I run to meet them. "No peeking!" I say as I blindfold our moms.

Mary Ann's mom pats her belly. "Careful!" she says.

"Don't worry," Mary Ann and I say at the same time. Since Colleen's baby is due this summer, *careful* is a word she uses a lot.

We guide our moms to the chairs we set up at the wish pond. We sit them down. Then we take off the blindfolds. "Wow!" both moms say as they look at the table of treats in front of them. Mary Ann and I adjust the pillows behind their backs to make sure they are extra comfy.

Mary Ann's mom smiles. "What did we do to deserve all this?" she asks.

"Eat first, talk later," I say. Mary Ann and I serve our moms cupcakes, fruit, and lemonade. When they're done eating, we offer them each a mint.

Then they look at us like it's time to start talking.

Mary Ann gives me a *you're-the-spokesperson-of-this-operation* look.

I clear my throat and start. The first part of what I have to say is easy. I remind our moms about the contest we entered. I show them the letters from Fashion Fran.

"Mallory, you won the contest? That's wonderful!" Colleen gushes.

"I'm so proud of you, Mallory!" My mom gives me a huge hug.

I wait while they read the letter. I keep waiting while they talk about how exciting it is to have won a contest. Then I pause. The next thing I have to say is not so easy to say.

"Mary Ann and I want to go to New York together, with the two of you."

Both moms look at each other like they are not sure about that.

Mom takes the letter addressed to my parents and starts reading. Colleen shifts around in her chair like she is uncomfortable. Before either of them have a chance to say anything, I keep talking.

I explain how Mary Ann and I entered this contest together. I tell them how we have never been on a mother-daughter trip with just the four of us. I remind them that once Mary Ann's mom has the baby, it would be a very long time before we could think about going on a mother-daughter trip together.

Both moms shake their heads like that is not something that is going to happen.

Then they both start firing off questions faster than kernels pop out of the popcorn machine at the movie theater.

Mom looks at me. "Mallory, have you thought about Dad and Max? Don't you think they will want to go to New York too?" She shakes her head like she can't believe I didn't think of these things.

Colleen looks at Mary Ann. "Have you forgotten that I'm having a baby? How could I possibly keep up with you girls in New York?" She shakes her head like just the idea of it is tiring.

Mary Ann and I had a feeling this was how they were going to respond. We look at each other, and then we both pull lists out of our back pockets.

We start reading together.

10 Reasons Why We, Mallory and Mary Ann, Think You Should Take Your Daughters On a Trip to New York City Together!

Reason #1: It will be educational. (Don't you want your daughters to be educated?)

Reason #2: It will be exciting. (Don't you like excitement?)

Reason #3: It will be good bonding time with your daughters. (Daughter bonding is good!)

Reason #4: It will be the last chance for you (Colleen) to go on a trip with your daughter (Mary Ann) before your baby is born.

Reason #5: It will be the last chance for you (Sherry) to go on a trip with your daughter (Mallory) before Colleen's baby is born.

Reason #6: If you go on this trip to New York, you will not have to make any beds. (Someone in the hotel will do that for you.)

Reason #7: If you go on this trip to New York, you will not have to make dinner. (Someone in the hotel will do that for you too.)

Reason #8: If you go on this trip to New York, you will not have to feed your pets. (The hotel in New York does not allow pets, so you will leave yours at home and someone else will have to feed them.)

Reason #9: This trip will be FUN for your daughters. (Don't you want your daughters to have fun?)

Reason #10: This trip will be FUN for you. (Don't you want to have fun?)

Even though we said there were only 10 reasons why we think you should take your daughters to New York, there is a very important eleventh reason.

VERY IMPORTANT REASON #11: It is a once-in-a-lifetime opportunity to have a mother-daughter sleepover party all in the same room, all in one of the most exciting cities in the world.

Our moms look at the list, and then they look at us like they're not sure what to say. Even though I'm the official spokesperson, Mary Ann starts talking.

"Please, please, please!" she says. "Please say yes that we can all go together to New York."

Mary Ann gives me a *make-your-sad-puppy-face* look.

I make the best sad-puppy face I've ever made.

Our moms start talking quietly to each other. Even though we're close by, it is hard to tell what they are saying. I hear buzz words like *plane* and *hotel* and *timing*. But it is

Who could resist this face?

impossible to tell by their facial expressions if they are going to say "yes" or "no" to what we asked.

Mary Ann and I aren't taking any chances.

We came prepared. While our moms keep talking, Mary Ann and I hold up pictures of places to visit in New York City. We hold up pictures of the Empire State Building, the Statue of Liberty, Central Park, and Times Square.

Our moms look at the pictures, and then they look back at each other. I try to send a message from my brain to their brains to say yes.

Our moms keep talking quietly for what feels like a very long time.

Finally, they nod at each other like they agree.

Mary Ann grabs my hand. I feel like we

are in court and the jury is about to read their verdict. I squeeze Mary Ann's hand.

I don't think I can wait another second. And I don't have to.

"Girls," says Mom. "Pack your bags. We're going to New York!"

NEW YORK, NEW YORK

"So . . . what should our brilliant plan be for getting both of us on TV?" Mary Ann whispers into my ear for what seems like the three-thousandth time since our plane took off this morning.

I don't blame Mary Ann for wanting to get that figured out. I'm nervous about it too. But it's not what I want to think about right now. We just landed in New

York. There are so many cool things to see and do. I shove the tourist brochure that Fran's assistant sent to me into Mary Ann's hand and point to a picture of a horse and carriage. "Do you think we should take a ride around Central Park?" I ask, ignoring the question Mary Ann asked me.

But Mary Ann ignores the brochure. Her suitcase bumps into my leg as we exit the plane, and she asks her question again.

I know I need to answer her question. But I don't have a good answer.

As we walk out of the airport, I repeat the schedule that Mom told me this morning. "We're going to check into the hotel. Eat lunch. Then we're going to go to Fran's studio."

Mary Ann smiles when I say that like a visit to Fran's studio is the answer to our problems. "I'm sure you can work things out when we get there," she says.

It feels like the bag of pretzels and can of soda I had on the airplane are stuck in my throat. It doesn't seem fair that I'm the one in charge of figuring this out, but I feel like I am. "I'll try," I tell Mary Ann. Even though designing a winning outfit and getting our moms to bring us both to New York was hard, now that we're here, I feel like the hard part is just beginning.

Mary Ann and I follow our moms to a yellow taxi that her mom says will take us to our hotel. She also says that we're going to be amazed when we get there because New York City has everything.

"Do they have a wish pond?" I ask.

Both of our moms laugh.

"I don't think they have that," says Mary Ann's mom.

That's too bad because that is the one

thing I could use right now. As we leave the airport behind, I close my eyes and pretend like I'm at the wish pond on my street. I make a wish.

I wish I will figure out a way to get Mary Ann on Fashion Fran *with me.*

I keep my eyes closed for an extra-long time. I really want my wish to come true. I know Mary Ann wants to be on the show. I do too. I want us to both be on the show. Together.

I open my eyes when I feel someone's hand on my shoulder. "Mallory, look out the window," says Mom. She points to row after row of tall buildings.

Mary Ann and I both lean forward to get a better view.

I tap our taxi driver on the shoulder. "Is that New York City?" I ask pointing out his windshield.

"That's the East River," he says. "And that's the city in front of us."

"Wow!" I say. "I've never seen so many skyscrapers!"

"Wow! Wow! Wow! Wow! Wow!" Mary Ann says. She told me she's going to say one *"Wow!"* for each skyscraper she sees. But she stops after sixteen *"Wows!"*

"There are so many skyscrapers, I'd spend the whole trip saying *wow*," she says.

Both our moms laugh and so does our taxi driver.

I take a deep breath. I'm starting to feel like this trip is going to be a lot of fun. The sights of New York City are so exciting, and I am glad they are making Mary Ann think about something else besides the show.

There's so much to see as we drive through the streets of New York. "I've never seen so many stores or buildings or cars," I say.

"Or people!" says Mary Ann.

She's right. "There are people everywhere you look!" I say. There are people walking on the sidewalks, coming out of buildings, riding bicycles, and crossing streets.

"You'll see people out and about twenty-four hours a day," says our taxi driver. "New York is known as the city that never sleeps."

I dig in my purse and pull out my camera. "We're going to have to take a lot of pictures," I say to Mary Ann. I roll down the window and start snapping shots from the taxi.

Mary Ann takes out her camera and starts taking pictures too. "Our New York City scrapbook is going to be our biggest one ever!"

Everything that is going on outside our taxi is so exciting. New York is completely different from Fern Falls. We take pictures until our taxi stops in front of our hotel.

"We're here!" says Mom.

Small Town vs. Big City

Mary Ann's mom pays the taxi driver. We all get out of the taxi and get our suitcases.

"I can't believe we're really in New York!" says Mary Ann. I can't either. We start jumping up and down on the sidewalk. We scream together, "We're here! We're here! We're here!" I'm feeling happier by the minute.

Lots of people pass us while we're jumping and screaming, but no one seems to be paying any attention to us. Except our moms.

"Come on, girls," says my mom.

We follow her into the hotel.

"This place is awesome!" says Mary Ann when we get inside.

She's right. It's more than awesome. I look up. The ceilings are higher than my house. The lobby is filled with fluffy couches, fancy rugs, and vases of flowers.

"Let's check in and take the bags to the room," says my mom. "We can all freshen up, and then we'll get some lunch and go to the studio,"

When she says "go to the studio," I look at Mary Ann. I know I should be thinking about what we're going to do when we get there. But I'm not. And I can tell Mary Ann isn't either. It's hard to think about anything except how exciting it is to be in New York.

I feel like a candy dish. The only difference is that I'm filled up with happiness, not mints or jelly beans.

Mary Ann and I walk around the lobby while our moms talk to a lady behind the desk. Then we follow them into an elevator and up to the twenty-fourth floor.

When we get inside our room, I can't

believe what I'm seeing. There are two huge beds covered in fluffy pillows. There's a big window with long, fancy curtains. And behind another door is a marble bathroom with an oversized bathtub. But the best thing in our room is a big basket of fruit and candy on the desk. The card with it says: *To Miss Mallory McDonald.* I open it and start reading.

To Miss Mallory McDonald,
Welcome to New York!
See you on the set.
Fashionably,
Fran

"Wow!" I say. I pop a chocolate into my mouth. I don't know if it is because they're from Fran or because we're in New York and candy tastes extra good here, but it is the best chocolate I've ever had.

Mary Ann eats a chocolate too. She goes

to the window and looks outside. "Wow!" she says. "Mallory, you have to see this!"

I go to the window and look out. There is an incredible view of New York City outside our window. I can look into some buildings and see the tops of other ones. "Wow!" I say. "I've never slept so high up."

Our moms look at each other. "Wow!" they say at the same time. Mary Ann's mom and my mom start laughing. "You girls sound like parrots who only know one word," says Colleen.

We might sound like parrots, but I can't think of a better word to describe everything. New York is *WOW!*

I hop on the bed and start jumping. "Wow! Wow! Wow!"

Mary Ann hops on the bed and starts jumping with me. "Wow! Wow! Wow!" she repeats.

We hold hands while we jump.

We both fall down on the bed on top of the big fluffy pillows and start laughing.

Being in New York is so exciting. I was worried this morning, but now I feel just one thing, and I can tell my best friend feels the same thing: happy.

I feel happy.

Happy! Happy! Happy!

THE UNHAPPY LIST

As happy as I was in the hotel, I am just as unhappy now. And I am not the only one who is unhappy. Mary Ann is unhappy too. In fact, if there was a list called the Unhappy List, both of our names would be on it.

Here's why:

When we first got to Fran's studio, everything was perfect.

A nice man named Ernesto gave us all a tour of the set.

We got to go backstage.

We saw the sewing room.

We saw Fran's dressing room.

We got to walk through the photo gallery of Fran's most fashionable looks.

We even got to have chocolate-covered strawberries and fresh-squeezed orange juice in Fran's personal snack lounge.

Everything was perfect until Ernesto took us to meet Fran's assistant, Holiday. We went with our moms to Holiday's office to discuss "show day details."

That was when everything went from perfect to NOT.

First, Holiday explained what would happen on the day of the show. She talked about where I would need to be and what I would need to do. My mom asked lots of questions. I shifted around in my chair and tried to listen while Holiday went over the details.

Wardrobe.

Fitting.

Stage.

Model.

Dream outfit.

I tried to focus while Holiday explained that I would have to be backstage early.

Mom, Colleen, and Mary Ann would all have front row seats in the audience. I even heard her say something about giving them special backstage passes for after the show.

But as exciting as it all was, it was hard to focus on what Holiday was saying when I had something of my own to say. I crossed my toes that what I was about to say would work.

When Holiday stopped talking, I started.

I explained to Holiday how Mary Ann and I are lifelong best friends. I told her how we worked on our designs together and how we entered the contest together. I told her that we like to do everything together and that we would like to be on the *Fashion Fran* show. TOGETHER!

I thought I said it all very convincingly.

Even Mary Ann gave me a look like I had

done a good job.

So I smiled and waited for Holiday to say something like, *"I get it. I've got a lifelong best friend too. If we won a contest to be on TV, we'd want to do it together too. Not a problem. You girls will be adorable together on TV."*

But that's not what Holiday said.

All she said was, "Sorry, girls. Mallory won the contest." As if it was something we should've already known.

Then she pushed her chair back from her desk. She took a deep breath and looked at her watch like what I was saying was not something she had time to deal with.

Portrait of a Grumpy Assistant

My mom and Colleen looked at each other and shook their heads. They apologized to Holiday and said something about how they hadn't known I would ask such a thing.

At that point, I gave Mary Ann an *I-don't-know-what-else-to-do* look.

Mary Ann gave me a *make-your-sad-puppy-face* look.

I made it.

But it didn't work.

That's when I tried dabbing my eyes like the idea of Mary Ann not going on the show with me was enough to make me cry.

Even Mary Ann looked like she was going to cry.

But that didn't work either.

Holiday just shook her head. "Girls, only Mallory can go on the show. It wouldn't be fair to everyone else who entered the contest if we bent the rules. I'm sorry, but modeling on *Fashion Fran* is not something the two of you will be able to do together."

Then Holiday looked at her watch again and stood up. Our moms stood up too. I knew it meant the meeting was over.

But Mary Ann and I just slumped down in our chairs and looked at each other.

Like I said, both of our names belonged on the Unhappy List.

THE QUIET GAME

Ever since we left Fran's studio yesterday, Mary Ann and I have been doing two things.

Thing One: Seeing New York.

Thing Two: Playing the Quiet Game.

Actually, we have been doing a third thing, which is fighting. But I can't tell you about the third thing until I tell you about the first two.

It's not hard to figure out why we were doing the first thing, which was seeing New York.

The reason we were doing the second thing—playing the Quiet Game—was because Mary Ann was not speaking to me.

It started when we left Fran's studio. Mary Ann said we would have to think of a way she could be on the show with me.

I told Mary Ann I didn't think we could do that. I reminded her that I already asked Holiday if she could be on the show with me, and Holiday said no.

Even our moms said it was silly to keep talking about this.

But it was the only thing Mary Ann wanted to talk about.

So I explained again that I tried talking to Holiday. I told her I made my best sad puppy face. I reminded her that I even pretended to cry and that nothing I did worked.

I didn't know what else we could do.

Then Mary Ann got mad.

She said something about "trying harder" and not speaking to friends who don't keep their pinky swears. And that's when she stopped speaking to me. Since she stopped speaking to me, I had no choice but to stop speaking to her.

So, like I said, we played the Quiet Game. We played it the whole time we were seeing New York. Which, to be honest, did not make seeing New York as much fun as it should have been. We kept playing the Quiet Game until we started fighting.

Keep reading and you'll see what I mean.

THE STATUE OF LIBERTY

The first place we went was the Statue of Liberty. We took a ferry to get there.

Once we arrived, we took a tour of Liberty Island. We ate in the restaurant and shopped in the gift store. We bought Statue of Liberty snow globes for Max and Joey and Winnie. We bought postcards for ourselves. We took lots of pictures.

Sounds like fun, right? Not exactly.

While we were ferrying and touring and eating and shopping and photographing, we were also not saying a word to each other.

And that made our moms mad.

They said that while we were at the Statue of Liberty, we should not be thinking about a TV show. We should be thinking about things like freedom and liberty and justice for all.

I said (to our moms, not to Mary Ann) that we *were* thinking about those things. We just weren't talking about them.

Then Mary Ann said (to our moms and not directly to me, but I think she wanted me to hear what she was saying) that all people should have the liberty and freedom to go on TV with their best friend.

The Speaking Chart

←Not Speaking to each other→

ONLY
Speaking to them

TIMES SQUARE

We also went to Times Square.

When we got there, Mary Ann and I looked at all the lights and signs, and believe me, there are a lot of lights

and signs to look at. We watched a group of actors perform a song from a musical. We went into what I am sure is the largest Toys "R" Us on the planet, and we got to ride a real Ferris wheel and eat in a real ice-cream parlor inside the store.

Sounds great, right?

Not completely.

All of this looking and watching and riding and eating would have been great, except that while Mary Ann and I were doing all of this, we were not saying a word. At least, not to each other.

My mom said that all of this not talking was getting ridiculous.

Mary Ann's mom said that we were ruining the trip of a lifetime.

But even though they said these things, Mary Ann still would not talk to me, so I had no choice but to still not talk to her.

CENTRAL PARK

Another famous place we visited was Central Park. It is a very old, beautiful park. There are lots of trees and flowers and statues and fountains. There is a zoo, and there are horse-drawn carriages that will take you on a ride through the park.

I bet you are thinking that it would be really hard to do anything but have fun when we were surrounded by trees and

flowers and statues and fountains and a zoo, and taking a horse-drawn carriage ride (which is what we did) through the park.

But if that is what you thought, you thought wrong.

While we were doing all of that stuff at Central Park, Mary Ann and I were still not talking to each other.

I actually tried talking to her.

While we were on the horse-drawn carriage ride, I told her that I was sorry it did not work out that we could both go on the show. I told her that I really wanted us to both go on the show together. I told her I would NEVER break a pinky swear, but this is one that is not possible to keep.

When I said that, Mary Ann just looked the other way. I think it was her way of saying (or not saying) that she was very upset.

To be honest, I was starting to get just as upset as she was.

JOHNNY'S FAMOUS PIZZA

That's when the Quiet Game we were playing ended. And the fighting started.

When we left Central Park, we went to Johnny's Pizza for lunch.

Johnny's Pizza was filled with tables

covered with red-checkered tablecloths. The restaurant was packed with people eating pizza that looked and smelled delicious. Mary Ann and I got in line with our moms to order our pizza.

When it was our turn to order, I said, "Let's get mushroom."

Mary Ann said, "I want pepperoni."

"I said, "You love mushroom."

Mary Ann crossed her arms across her chest. "Not anymore," she said. "I can't stand mushrooms on my pizza." Then she made a face like just the idea of mushrooms on pizza was enough to make her sick.

And that's when I got mad. Really mad! Mary Ann has been eating mushrooms on pizza for as long as I can remember. It seemed to me that someone who had been eating

mushrooms all of their life wouldn't
suddenly stop liking mushrooms.

"I'm sorry that you don't get to go on
the *Fashion Fran* show," I said in more of an
outside voice than an inside voice.

People in line started to look at me, but
I kept using my outside voice. "I tried to
work it out!" I said to Mary Ann loudly. "But
I couldn't. We are in New York, and you are
ruining the trip by not talking to me!"

Then Mary Ann said, "I might not be
talking to you, but you are yelling at me!"

That's when we started yelling at each other. I don't even remember what we were yelling. I just remember that our moms grabbed us by the arms and marched us out of Johnny's Pizza.

They said lots of stuff about how we were in New York and there are a lot of enjoyable sights to see, but a sight they did not want to see was the sight of the two of us not getting along. Then we all got into a taxi and went back to our hotel.

Mary Ann and I didn't get to eat the pizza that looked and smelled delicious. And to make matters worse, our moms made us say "I'm sorry" to each other for fighting. Then they said that until we could speak nicely to each other, we should go back to not speaking at all.

Unfortunately, the Quiet Game is not a fun game. Especially on an empty stomach.

THE GIRL WHO HAD IT ALL, ALMOST

A True Tale By Mallory McDonald

Once upon a time there was a girl who had it all, almost.

She was cute. At least, that's what people told her.

CUTE!

She was smart. Well, pretty smart, according to her teacher and her report card.

She was funny and had a sweet nature and a good sense of style. (No one actually said these things, but in her heart, she believed they were true.)

She had a mom and a dad and a brother and a cat and a dog.

She had her own room and her own bathroom (sort of). She had to share the bathroom with her brother, but she always tried her hardest to pretend she didn't so it was almost like she had her own.

She had a lot of joke books and a lot of colors of nail polish.

She was a good cook (at least when it came to making peanut butter and marshmallow sandwiches and chocolate chip cookies).

She lived on a street with her very own wish pond, and she lived next door to her very best friend.

To top things off, the girl won a fashion design contest and got to go on a trip to New York and appear on her favorite TV show. She got to bring her mom and her best friend's mom and her best friend with her.

You are probably reading this and thinking: "Wow! This girl has it all! I don't get the ALMOST part. What in the world doesn't she have?"

Well, since I am the girl writing the story and the story is about me, I will answer that question.

What the girl didn't have was a happy best friend.

And this made the girl unhappy too.

The reason the girl's best friend wasn't happy was because she was not going to get to be on the TV show with the girl. Since they have always been best friends, they have always tried to do everything together. They tried to go on the TV show together, but it didn't work out the way it was supposed to.

The girl tried to make it work out.

She tried really hard to make it work out. Really, really, really hard.

But nothing she did worked. And to make matters worse, she had promised her best friend that they would make it work out. She had even pinky-sworn that they would make it work out. The girl was the type of girl who always tried to keep her pinky swears, but she was having a hard time keeping this one.

Portrait of a girl who always keeps her pinky swears.

And it was making the trip to New York, which was supposed to be amazing, not so amazing at all.

The girl's best friend was very upset with her.

In fact, she had hardly spoken to the girl the whole trip, and this very afternoon, they had had a big fight at a pizza restaurant. Even though she and the girl made up after their fight (mostly because their moms made them), she hasn't said much to the girl all day.

Now it's the end of the day.

The girls are in bed at their beautiful, luxurious hotel in New York City. They are propped up against fluffy pillows. The girl is writing this story in her journal. The girls' best friend is pretending to read a fashion magazine.

The reason the girl knows her best friend is pretending to read the magazine is because there are big tears in her eyes and everyone knows it is impossible to read fashion magazines when your eyes are filled with tears.

This is making the girl very sad.

She knows her best friend is crying because tomorrow, the girl is going to be on national TV, on their favorite show, modeling the winning outfit she designed. While she is doing that, her best friend will be sitting in the studio audience.

She would like her best friend to be going on national TV with her, but that is not going to happen.

She would also like to be talking to her best friend about how excited she is to be going on national TV tomorrow. But that is not going to happen either.

So that is why the girl has it all . . . almost.

AN IDEA

Last night, there was something I, Mallory McDonald, didn't get, and that thing was sleep.

When Mary Ann closed her eyes, I could not close mine. All I could think about was how upset Mary Ann was. I really wanted to figure out a way for her to go on *Fashion Fran* with me. But I could not think of a way.

I laid in bed for a long time trying to think of a way. I even pretended that I was

at the wish pond and remade the wish that
I made when we were in the taxi on the
way into the city.

*I wish I could figure out a way to get Mary
Ann on the* Fashion Fran *show.*

Then I tried to close my eyes and go to
sleep, but it felt like my brain would not
let me.

This morning, I
woke up just as the
sun was coming up.
I don't know when
it happened. But
sometime between last
night and this morning,
I came up with an idea.

I think it might be a
great idea.

At least, I hope it is. It is the only idea I
could think of.

I shake Mary Ann's shoulder. "Wake up," I whisper.

As soon as Mary Ann finishes rubbing her eyes, I start talking. Actually, I start whispering. Even though our moms look like they are still sleeping, I don't want to take any chances. I don't want Mom and Colleen to hear what I have to say.

I whisper my idea into Mary Ann's ear.

It's really more of a plan than an idea. It takes me a while to whisper my plan into Mary Ann's ear because it is a plan with a lot of parts. It is also a plan that will fail if every part doesn't go according to plan.

When I'm done whispering, Mary Ann looks at me like I just invented a way to make spinach taste good. "You're a genius!" she whispers.

I don't think I'm a genius, but hopefully my plan will work. I don't know what else will.

Mary Ann gives me a serious look. "You would really do that for me?"

I nod. "We're best friends," I whisper. "And we made a pinky swear."

Mary Ann grins. "You're not my best friend. You're my best, best, best friend." Then she stops grinning. "Do you really think we can pull this off?" she asks quietly.

The truth is . . . I don't know if my plan will work. But I don't know what else will either. "If anyone can make it work, we can," I say to Mary Ann. "But it won't be easy."

We cross our fingers on both of our hands.

Right when we do, the alarm goes off in our room. Mom yawns. "Rise and shine," she says. "We need to get to the studio early."

Colleen looks at the clock. "This is so exciting! Mallory, in a few hours you will be on national television."

"Right," I say to Colleen. Then I wink the tiniest wink at Mary Ann.

Hopefully, in a few hours, Mary Ann and I will both be on national television.

SHOWTIME

"Let's get a move on!" says Holiday when we arrive at the studio.

She takes my arm. "You're coming backstage with me." She motions to Mary Ann and our moms. "Ernesto will show the three of you to your seats in the audience." She hands Mom the backstage passes for the three of them after the show.

Holiday starts to lead me backstage, but

I stop. It's time to put my plan into action.

I cross my toes. "Um, Holiday, I'm a little nervous," I say. I try to look nervous, which isn't too hard because I actually *am* nervous.

Holiday rolls her eyes. "We're on a schedule." She tries again to get me to walk with her, but I don't budge.

My nervous face

I put my hand on my stomach and bend over a little. I make a face like I'm really, really nervous and my nerves might make me sick. "I'd feel a whole lot better if my best friend could stay backstage with me."

Mary Ann rubs my arm and then looks at Holiday. "Trust me, you don't want to see what happens when she gets nervous."

Mary Ann gives a little demonstration of what might happen.

Our moms look like they are about to say something like, *"Girls, you need to do what Holiday says."*

Avoid at all costs!

But before they can say anything, Holiday grabs Mary Ann's arm too. "C'mon, we don't have time for this." She leads us both backstage.

Mary Ann and I silently high-five each other. So far, so good.

As we walk, Holiday looks at Mary Ann

and me. "You two look like twins."

We give each other a teensy, tiny *what-we're-doing-seems-to-be-working* wink. Part of our plan was to look the same. Even our moms said this morning that it was hard to tell us apart.

We both have on jeans and black, long-sleeved T-shirts. We both have our hair tucked into baseball caps. We're both wearing dark sunglasses.

We silently high-five each other again. Our plan is going as planned.

When we get backstage, Holiday leads us to the wardrobe room. She motions for Mary Ann to sit in a chair. She puts me in front of a bunch of mirrors. "It's time to get you dressed for the show," she says.

Seamstresses swarm around me like bees. They dress me in the dream outfit that I designed.

Holiday tells me to stand still while
they make adjustments. She says not to
move while they put on my wig, hat, and
sunglasses.

When they're done, I look in the mirror.

I can't believe how good my dream outfit looks. I also can't believe what a good idea it was to add the wig, hat, and sunglasses.

I look over my shoulder at Mary Ann. She gives me a thumbs-up.

Holiday grabs my arm. "Let's go," she says. "You're on in ten, and Fran wants to meet you."

I gulp. I can't wait to meet Fran, but it's going to have to wait a few minutes. The next step of my plan is very important. If it doesn't happen, nothing will work the way it is supposed to.

I take a deep breath, and then I raise my hand. "May I use the bathroom?" I ask Holiday.

Mary Ann raises her hand too. "May I use it too?"

Holiday shakes her head like she's had just about all she can take.

She points to a door. "It's over there. But make it quick."

Mary Ann and I walk toward the bathroom. As I do, I make a mental map of the area backstage. I whisper to

Mary Ann for her to do the same thing. It's important that we know where we're going.

Once we get inside the bathroom, I quickly go over things with Mary Ann. We don't have much time. She nods her head as I talk. "Got it," she says each time I pause.

"Got it."

"Got it."

"Got it."

Holiday knocks on the door. "The show starts in five. Fran is waiting."

Mary Ann squeezes my hand. "You're going to meet Fran!"

"So are you!" I link my arm through hers, and we walk out of the bathroom.

Holiday takes a deep breath and shakes her head. She leads us both back to the dressing room.

When we get there, someone is waiting for us, and that someone is Fran. I suck in my breath. She's even more fashionable in person than she is on TV.

"Hello, girls!" Fran smiles at us. She has the whitest teeth I've ever seen.

Neither Mary Ann nor I can speak. I can't even believe we are standing in the

same room with Fashion Fran. I'm sure
Mary Ann can't believe it either.

Fran laughs. "There's no place for
shyness in show biz," she says.

Holiday must have told Fran why Mary
Ann is backstage, but Fran doesn't seem
to mind. Fran winks at me. "Your outfit is
dreamy," she says with a big smile.

Before I even have a chance to say
"*thank you*," Holiday checks her watch. "Two

minutes and counting," she says.

Fran nods at me. "See you onstage."

The next thing I know, Holiday is going over the directions she gave me the other day in her office. It was hard to listen then, but now I am paying attention to every word she says. And so is Mary Ann.

"It's simple. Fran is going to introduce you. You walk out, smile, cross the stage, turn, pause, wave, and walk back. Then, we cut to a commercial. You will model your outfit one more time after the commercial. Got it?" Holiday asks.

I nod. I got it. I look at Mary Ann. She heard what Holiday said and nods at me like she got it too.

A red light starts blinking backstage.

"Showtime!" says Holiday.

What happens next is a blur.

Lights twinkle onstage. The familiar

music that plays at the beginning of each episode of *Fashion Fran* begins. The announcer who does the countdown starts to count.

The next thing I know, Fran is onstage.

She is talking.

She is laughing.

She is modeling an outfit.

Then I hear her telling the audience about the contest. I hear my name.

"GO!" Holiday mouths to me.

I can't tell if I'm excited or nervous or a mix of both.

I walk up the stairs onto the stage. When I do, I hear lots of clapping. I look out into the audience, but the lights are so bright, it is hard to see.

I do exactly what Holiday told me to do.

I walk across the stage and model the dream outfit I designed.

When I get to the far end, I turn and pause. I put my one hand on my hip and wave to the audience with my other hand.

There's lots of clapping.

I smile at the cameras and wave again. I might have been scared when I first walked onstage, but right now, I feel like modeling on my favorite TV show is the most exciting thing I've ever done. My tunic top, skinny jeans, jewelry, boots, glasses, hat, and wig feel very fashionable.

I keep smiling as I walk back across the stage.

When I get back to where I started, I walk down the steps. I hear Fran say we are cutting to a commercial break.

"Two minutes until we're back on air," Holiday says.

I look at Mary Ann and nod. I would love to tell my best friend how exciting it was to model on national television, but now is not the time for that.

Mary Ann and I have work to do, and not much time to do it.

I tap Holiday on the arm. "I have to go to the bathroom again," I tell her. I hold my stomach and make a face like this time, it's going to be a real problem if I don't.

Mary Ann loops her arm around me like it's her job to hold me up and if she weren't doing it, I'd be on the floor.

Holiday looks at her watch and shakes her head. "You better make it quick."

Mary Ann keeps her arm around me as we walk into the bathroom.

Let the switch up Begin!

When we get inside, Mary Ann and I nod at each other.

It is time to put the most important part of our plan into action.

I put on Mary Ann's black shirt, jeans, baseball cap, and sunglasses.

Mary Ann puts on my skinny jeans, tunic top, vest, bracelets, necklace, boots, hat, glasses, and wig.

We change clothes faster than my brother can change the TV channel to a game he wants to watch.

I straighten Mary Ann's necklace.

She tucks some stray hair into my baseball cap.

"I can't tell who's who," she says

Holiday bangs on the door. "Mallory, you're on."

I push my glasses back on my nose. With the baseball cap and glasses, it really is hard to tell Mary Ann and me apart.

Mary Ann fluffs up her wig. "How do I look?" she asks.

I stand back and inspect her. She looks just like I did two minutes ago. I nod like I approve. "Showtime," I whisper.

Mary Ann and I squeeze our hands together for luck.

Then I open the door.

DOUBLE
TROUBLE

I cross my toes that Holiday won't notice anything different, but Holiday is not in a noticing mood.

She grabs Mary Ann's arm and marches her to the side of the stage faster than Princess Jasmine crosses the sky on her magic carpet.

The red light backstage starts blinking again.

I look at Mary Ann. She looks just like I looked in my dream outfit. I just hope she can model like me too.

I can tell she's excited and nervous, just like I was. She turns around and looks at me. I give her a *you-can-do-it* look.

I can see the lights on the stage twinkling.

Fran starts talking to the audience and the cameras. "Welcome back to our very special Design Your Dream Outfit episode."

I listen as Fran talks about how many people entered the contest and how many good designs she looked at before she chose this one. "I'm going to ask our winner, Miss Mallory McDonald, to walk the stage one more time and model her creation."

Music starts playing again. It's Mary Ann's cue to start walking.

Holiday pushes Mary Ann up the stairs.

I cross my toes and my fingers as tightly as I've ever crossed them before. I hope we can pull this off. *"GO!"* I say silently. And she does.

I watch from backstage as Mary Ann walks across the stage. When she gets to the far end, she turns and pauses, just like I did.

She puts one hand on her hip and waves to the audience, just like I did.

The audience claps. She smiles at the camera and waves again. Then she walks back across the stage. Just like I did.

When she gets back to where Fran is standing, Fran wraps an arm around her. "Let's give a big round of applause to Miss Mallory McDonald."

I listen while the audience claps and the music keeps playing.

We did it! I let out a deep breath.

I can't believe I was on the *Fashion Fran* show and so was Mary Ann. Our dream came true. All our wishing and planning and pinky swearing worked.

"Isn't her outfit dreamy?" I hear Fran ask the audience.

There's more clapping, and then Fran talks some more about fashion and design.

When she's done she waves good-bye to the audience and says what she says at the end of every episode.

"That's it for today. See you tomorrow with more of the latest, greatest finds in the world of fashion." She blows a kiss.

Somewhere I hear a man yell, "Cut!"

The next thing I know, Mary Ann is walking down the steps back toward me.

As happy as I am and as much as I want to jump for joy with her that we were both on the *Fashion Fran* show, now is definitely not the time for that. There's one more part of my plan that needs to happen. And it's an important part, too: we need to change back before anyone notices we changed in the first place.

I give Mary Ann a *follow-me* look.

I walk toward the bathroom and so does

she. When we get inside, I close the door and lock it.

Mary Ann's skin is sparkly from the heat of the lights. "Your plan went off without a hitch!" she whispers. "I don't know what made you add the wig, hat, and glasses to your dream outfit, but if you hadn't, this plan never would have worked."

I don't know what made me add them either, but I'm glad I did!

Mary Ann hugs me. "We did it!" she says just loudly enough for me to hear.

"We're still doing it," I say.

She nods like she gets exactly what I mean.

I peel off my clothes and Mary Ann peels off hers. We change clothes even faster than we changed the first time, and I didn't think that was possible.

When we finish changing, Mary Ann and

I inspect each other. "Everything is just like it was before we changed," she whispers.

I nod that I agree.

Mary Ann and I both take deep breaths.

I have a feeling when we open this door, Holiday will be right there on the other side, waiting to take us to our mothers.

But I'm surprised when I open the door, and so is Mary Ann. Holiday is not the one who is waiting for us.

It's Fran. She looks at us with her hands on her hips.

"Girls," says Fran, "you are in double trouble!"

FACING FRAN

Fran walks us to her dressing room. She closes the door. It's just the three of us.

Fran's face is blank. It's hard to tell what she's thinking. I give Mary Ann a worried look, and she gives me the same look back.

"Girls, that was some switchup," says Fran.

I try to swallow, but it feels like there is a wad of gum stuck in my throat. "Are you mad at us?" I ask Fran.

Sometimes, when you ask a question, waiting to hear the answer is even scarier than asking the question. This is one of those times. She makes a *hmmm* sound. Then she taps her foot.

I feel like her *hmmm* and her foot tap mean she wants an explanation, so I give her one. I explain how Mary Ann and I are best friends and how we do everything together. I explain how one of the things we wanted to do together was to be on her show.

I pause. Then I look at Mary Ann like I need her help.

She picks up where I left off.

She explains to Fran how her show is our favorite. "We have watched it every day together our whole lives," Mary Ann tells Fran.

She keeps talking. "It has always been

our dream to be on your show. Together."
She looks down at her feet and shrugs
like what she's about to say next might
not make sense, but she hopes Fran
understands. "When Mallory won the
contest, we made a pinky swear that
somehow, some way, we would figure out
how to both be on your show."

I look at Mary Ann. Then she looks at me
like she's not sure what else we can say.

"We didn't mean to break the rules," I
say.

Mary Ann and I look at each other again.
"We're really sorry," we say at the same
time.

Fran looks from me to Mary Ann. She
studies us for a moment like she's trying to
figure out a complicated problem.

It feels like forever before she says
anything.

Finally, she does. "Apology accepted," says Fran.

She puts one arm around me and the other one around Mary Ann. "In fashion, creativity is the name of the game. You two certainly found a creative solution to your problem, and the show went off without a hitch."

Fran smiles. "I'm sure the two of you will

make excellent fashion designers one day. Actresses too. That was an almost flawless performance."

I scratch my head. Something doesn't make sense to me. I can tell Mary Ann is confused too.

"If it was an almost flawless performance, how did you know we switched places?" I ask Fran.

Fran smiles. "You can fool some of the people some of the time. But never Fashion Fran."

She looks at me. "When you turned, you waved with your right hand. Always a good indication that someone is a righty."

Then she looks at Mary Ann. "When you waved, you did it with your left hand." She pauses. "Sure sign of a lefty," she says.

Mary Ann and I look at each other and shrug. We thought of almost everything, but we never thought of that.

"You caught us," says Mary Ann.

Fran looks pleased with herself, like she's a detective who just figured out a mystery. "Even though we're best friends and a lot alike, we have one big difference. I'm right-handed and Mary Ann is left-handed," I say to Fran.

Fran laughs. "Even best friends have their differences."

Fran is right. Mary Ann and I might have our differences, but I know one thing we both feel the same way about is being sorry that we tried to fool Fashion Fran. We apologize again.

Fran holds up her hand like we can stop apologizing. "I don't like being fooled," says Fran. "But I understand the situation, and I applaud you both for finding such a creative solution. In show business, the bottom line is a good show. You girls put on a very good show."

She gives us both a kiss on the cheek. "It will be our secret."

I look at Mary Ann and she looks at me. We both put our hands on our cheeks at the same time.

I know Mary Ann and I have another thing in common now. Neither one of us is ever going to wash our cheeks again.

Ever!

ON TOP OF
THE WORLD

"Good-bye girls!" Fran waves and blows
a kiss as we leave the studio.

Mary Ann and I wave and blow kisses
back.

My mom and Colleen smile at each
other. They're happy now, but they weren't
so happy right after the show.

When they came backstage, they were
very upset that we switched places.

When we asked them how they knew, they just said mothers know everything.

I don't know if that is true, but I do know that Mary Ann and I had to have a very long talk with them about "deception." And that was even after Fran told them that she wasn't too upset with us, as the show went just fine. She says in show business, the only thing that matters is what the audience sees.

The good news is that we finished that talk. And we still have a few hours left in New York before we go back home.

Mary Ann and I walk behind our moms as we leave the studio.

"I still can't believe you figured out a way to get us both on *Fashion Fran!*" Mary Ann says to me.

She smiles and puts her arm around my shoulder. "Thanks again for what you did for me." Then she gets a serious look on her face. "I'm sorry we got in trouble with our moms, but it was like a dream coming true."

"No big deal," I say. "You would have done the same thing for me."

Mary Ann grins. "If we ever enter another contest, I will do exactly the same thing for you." She holds up her pinky. "Pinky swear."

But I shake my head. "No more pinky swears for a while," I say.

Mary Ann laughs and nods like she agrees.

Our moms stop walking and turn around. "We still have one more thing on the agenda before we head home," says my mom.

"The Empire State Building!" Mary Ann and I say at the same time.

I don't know how we could have forgotten! I point up in the sky. It's easy to see the Empire State Building from where we are. "Can we walk?"

Mom takes the city map out of her purse and studies it for a moment. "It's not too far. I don't see why not," she says.

As we walk, Mary Ann and I talk
and point to things in store windows.
Computers. Shoes. Clothes. Suitcases.
Even air conditioners. No wish ponds, but
anything else you might ever want is in
New York.

There are so many things to see. "I don't
think I could ever get bored of window
shopping here," I say to Mary Ann.

"You might get bored of waiting in line,"
she says.

She points to a long line of people
waiting outside the Empire State Building.
"Do you think they're all waiting to go to
the top?" asks Mary Ann.

"I'm afraid so," says Mary Ann's mom.

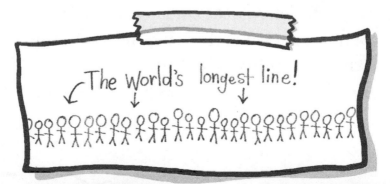

The World's longest line!

She opens her New York City guidebook and starts reading. "Between ten and twenty thousand people visit the Empire State Building every day."

We get in line behind a family with six kids who all have on matching red T-shirts and baseball caps. There are all kinds of families and groups of schoolkids. There are two old people holding hands. I wonder if they have been waiting their whole lives to visit this place. I look at the crowd. There are so many different kinds of people waiting to see the Empire State Building.

My teacher, Mr. Knight, taught us that the United States is often referred to as the Great Melting Pot because so many people from different places came to live in this country, and when they did, their cultures all blended together a little. He said another term for having lots of different kinds of people is cultural diversity. I think I've seen more cultural diversity in New York than anywhere else I've ever been.

"I don't think we'll get too bored in line," I say to Mary Ann. "Looking at all the people in New York is even more interesting than looking in the store windows."

Mary Ann nods like she agrees.

As we get closer to the front of the line, Mary Ann starts hopping up and down. "It's almost our turn," she squeals.

I'm just as excited as she is. We go through the security line and wait until, finally, it's our turn to get into the elevator. I can feel my ears pop as the elevator moves upward. It takes us to the eightieth floor.

When we get out, there's an exhibit on the history of the Empire State Building.

"It's like a museum in here," says Mary Ann.

It really is. There are Empire State Building facts and photos everywhere. Best of all, there's a gift shop. Mary Ann and I buy small models of the Empire State Building to take home to Max and Joey and Winnie.

"Ready to go to the observation deck?" Mom asks when we're done shopping.

"We're ready!" Mary Ann and I say at the same time.

We follow our moms on to another elevator that takes us to the eighty-sixth floor. When we get out, we are looking over what seems like the entire world.

"Wow! Wow! Wow!" screams Mary Ann. "This is cool!"

It really is. I don't even know where to look first. There's a tall glass wall that wraps around the whole deck. You can walk along each side of the deck and see New York from all four directions. There are people everywhere, but I don't care and neither does Mary Ann.

"You can walk around all four sides of the deck," says Mom.

We start walking and looking. We squeeze ourselves in between groups of people to get a look at all the different views of the city.

You can see everything from up here. Buildings, bridges, parks, rivers, cars, and people. Even other states! There are big binoculars so that you can look more closely at things that are far away.

"I can't believe what I'm seeing!" I say to Mary Ann.

"I know," says Mary Ann. "It's so different from Fern Falls."

I laugh. "I think the highest building in Fern Falls is five floors. I can't believe we're eighty-six stories up in the air."

Mary Ann wraps her arms around her chest. "It's windy up here."

"Very windy!" I say as I try to tuck a piece of hair behind my ear. It keeps blowing in my face.

"We should take pictures," says Mary Ann.

She gets out her camera and gives it to her mom. We pose in different spots as Colleen snaps photos of us on top of the Empire State Building.

When we're done taking pictures, Mary Ann stretches out her arms. "I feel like I'm on top of the world," she smiles into the wind.

I know exactly how she feels. Last year, Mrs. Daily taught us the expression *on top of the world*. She said it means a feeling of complete happiness. Right now, I feel like I'm on top of the world in more ways than one.

I met my favorite TV star. Mary Ann and I both got to be on her show. We're in New York City. And now, I'm standing on top of the Empire State Building.

I really do feel like I'm on top of the world.

I close my eyes and try to take a mental picture of all this that I can keep in my brain forever.

A few minutes later, Mom taps me on the shoulder. "Time to go," she says.

I think she can tell I'm disappointed that we are leaving today. She wraps an arm around my shoulder. "One more stop before we go to the airport," she says.

"Where are we going?" I ask. But Mom won't say.

"One last little treat for you and Mary Ann," Colleen says as our taxi stops in front of Johnny's Famous Pizza.

"No one was in the mood for pizza the last time we came here." She winks at us. "Hopefully, this time it will be better."

Mary Ann and I race into Johnny's. We order a pizza.

"Pepperoni," I say.

"Mushroom," says Mary Ann.

"Pepperoni AND mushroom," we both say together and laugh.

When our pizza comes, we both take a bite. It is crispy, hot, and delicious.

"This is the best pizza I've ever had," says Mary Ann with her mouth stuffed full.

I agree completely. Mary Ann and I both eat a second slice.

"Why do you think pizza in New York is so good?" asks Mary Ann.

I look out the window at the cars and the people and the bikers and all the activity on the busy street. Some people say the pizza in New York is so good because of the water they use to make the dough. Personally, I think pizza tastes so good in New York because you are eating it in New York.

And the truth is . . . everything is fun in New York. Even eating pizza.

I stand up and put my paper plate in the trash.

It's time to say good-bye to the city that never sleeps.

FRIENDS FOREVER

"Ladies and Gentlemen, please fasten your seat belts. We'll be taking off shortly."

Mary Ann and I buckle our seat belts and sit back in our seats.

I look across the aisle at my mom and Mary Ann's mom. They're sitting next to each other, smiling and laughing, like one of them just told a funny joke. They look happy.

I look out the window. I wish I felt as happy as they seem. But I don't. Even though our trip to New York ended up being great, I feel sad that we're leaving. New York is such an exciting city, and there are so many things we didn't get to do.

As the plane lifts off, I press my nose against the window and look at the sites of New York. All the buildings are starting to look like miniatures. I try to locate some of the places we went.

It's easy to spot the Empire State Building. Johnny's Pizza is impossible to find.

I look under the seat in front of me at the bag of souvenirs I bought. Max will like the Statue of Liberty snow globe and mini Empire State Building I got him, but I really wish I could have brought him back a pizza from Johnny's. He would have loved that.

As the plane moves higher, the sites of the city start to disappear below the clouds. Our trip to New York is quickly becoming a memory.

Mary Ann leans toward me. "It's hard to believe it's all over, and we're on our way back to Fern Falls," she says.

It's almost like Mary Ann can read my mind.

"It makes me a little sad." I tell Mary Ann how much I loved going to New York. "It was so exciting and so different from home," I say.

I wait for Mary Ann to say she's sad too and that there's no place like New York. But her answer surprises me.

"I loved New York too," says Mary Ann. "But honestly, I'm happy to be going home."

I think about what she just said. I remind Mary Ann about the hotel we stayed in, the sites we saw, the food we ate, the busy streets we walked on, meeting Fashion Fran, and being on national TV. "Everything we did was so exciting." I shrug my shoulders. "Won't you miss all those things?" I ask Mary Ann.

Mary Ann is quiet for a minute.

"I will miss all those things," she says slowly like she's putting a lot of thought into choosing her words. "But I'm going home with my favorite thing."

I think about the things she bought at the airport gift shop.

She's taking home an I LOVE NY back scratcher for Joey, a Big Apple poster for

Winnie, and toe socks for herself.

I give Mary Ann an *I'm-not-sure-what-your-favorite-thing-you're-taking-home-is* look.

Mary Ann leans her head back against the seat and laughs. "My favorite thing I'm taking home is my best friend."

When Mary Ann says that, the engine rumbles and the plane shakes from side to side. The captain makes an announcement about hitting some turbulence and making sure our seat belts are buckled. My stomach feels like it is falling out of my body.

Mary Ann puts her hand on my arm like she can sense that I don't like the shaky-plane feeling.

"Thanks again for keeping the pinky swear we made and figuring out a way to get us both on the *Fashion Fran* show.

You're the best friend a girl could ask for," she says. "As long as we're together. I'm happy wherever I am."

I thought I was happy walking the streets of New York and meeting Fashion Fran and being on national TV and standing on top of the Empire State Building, but none of that felt as good as what Mary Ann just said.

The plane levels out and I take a deep breath.

Mary Ann has been my best friend since the day I was born. We've done so many fun things together over the years. Going to New York was definitely one of the most fun, but Mary Ann is right. As long as we're together, it doesn't really matter what we're doing.

I look at Mary Ann. Then I hold up my pinky. "I know I said no more, but do you want to make another pinky swear?" I ask.

She nods.

"Best friends forever," I say.

Mary Ann hooks her pinky around mine. "And ever," she says.

We smile at each other and squeeze our pinkies tightly together.

We both know this is one pinky swear that won't be hard to keep.

A SUPERSIZED SCRAPBOOK

Mary Ann and I have made a lot of scrapbooks over the years, but the scrapbook we made from our trip to New York is our biggest one ever.

When Mom saw it, she said it's SUPERSIZED, just like New York City. And she's right. We just had so many good pictures to put in it! It was really hard to choose, but here are some of my favorites.

Mary Ann and I at the hotel

Mary Ann and I in front of the Manhattan skyline

Mary Ann and I with Fashion Fran

And Mary Ann and I on top of the Empire
State Building

If you ask Mary Ann or me, we would
both tell you that we loved New York City.
But here's the funny thing about our trip:
even though not every minute of it was
perfect, when we look at our pictures, Mary
Ann and I agree it was all good because we
did it together.

Mom says things are always good
when you're doing them with someone
you care about.

I will say this: I don't always agree with my mother, but this time, I, Mallory McDonald, officially think she is right.

I'll say one more thing too. And since Mary Ann is standing right here beside me, we'll say it together: We officially loved, loved, loved our trip to New York City!

PIZZA, MALLORY AND MARY ANN STYLE

You already know how much Mary Ann and I loved the pizza in New York. But we like it even better on Wish Pond Road. Especially when it's cookie pizza. We found this recipe in a magazine. If you've never had Cookie Pizza, you have to pinky swear to us that you will try it immediately.

We promise you will love, love, love it!

COOKIE PIZZA
Ingredients:
One roll of refrigerated chocolate chip
   cookie dough
Small marshmallows
m&m's

Directions:

Step 1: Heat oven to 350 degrees.

Step 2: Press dough into a pizza pan.

Step 3: Sprinkle with marshmallows and m&m's. Press them into the dough.

Step 4: Bake for 10-15 minutes.

Step 5: Let your cookie pizza cool for 5 minutes.

Step 6: Cut into slices. Serve with milk and enjoy!

Trust us when we tell you that you will have as much fun making this as you will eating it. Happy eating!

Big, huge hugs and kisses!
Mallory and Mary Ann

P.S. This pizza tastes even better if you make it with a friend. We promise!

Darby Creek
A division of Lerner Publishing Group, Inc.
241 First Avenue North
Minneapolis, MN 55401 U.S.A.

Website address: www.lernerbooks.com

The images in this book are used with the permission of: Cover background: © PhotoDisc Royalty Free by Getty Images.

Main body text set in LuMarcLL 14/20. Typeface provided by Linotype.

Library of Congress Cataloging-in-Publication Data

Friedman, Laurie B., 1964–
    Mallory and Mary Ann take New York / by Laurie Friedman ; illustrations by Jennifer Kalis.
      p. cm. — (Mallory ; #19)
    ISBN 978-0-7613-6074-2 (trade hard cover : alk. paper)
    [1. Fashion design—Fiction. 2. Contests—Fiction. 3. Promises—Fiction. 4. Best friends—Fiction. 5. Friendship—Fiction. 6. New York (N.Y.)—Fiction.]
    I. Kalis, Jennifer, ill. II. Title.
    PZ7.F89773Mad 2013
    [Fic]—dc23   2012019008

Manufactured in the United States of America
1 — BP — 12/31/12

J
Fic
FRI

Certified Chain of Custody
SUSTAINABLE FORESTRY INITIATIVE
Promoting Sustainable Forestry
www.sfiprogram.org
SFI-01268

SFI label applies to the text stock